EMILY BROWN and the THING

First published in 2007 by Orchard Books
First published in paperback in 2008

Text © Cressida Cowell 2007
Illustrations © Neal Layton 2007

ORCHARD BOOKS
338 Euston Road, London NW1 3BH

Orchard Books Australia
Level 17/207 Kent Street
Sydney, NSW 2000

The rights of Cressida Cowell to be identified as the author and of Neal Layton to be identified as the illustrator of this work have been asserted by them in accordance with the Copyright, Designs and Patents Act, 1988.

ISBN 978 1 84616 694 5
Printed in China

Designed by David Mackintosh

Orchard Books is a division of Hachette Children's Books, an Hachette UK company.
www.hachettelivre.co.uk

EMILY BROWN and the THING

written by Cressida Cowell

illustrated by Neal Layton

ORCHARD BOOKS

Once upon a time,
there was a little girl called Emily Brown
and an old grey rabbit called Stanley.

Emily Brown and Stanley were trying to get to sleep
after a busy day. But a noise was keeping them awake.
SPLISH! went the noise. SPLOSH! went the noise.
It seemed to be coming from the window.

There was a Thing sitting on the windowsill.
Large tears were dripping onto his pyjamas.

"Oh, Emily Brown, Emily Brown!" wept the Thing. "I can't find my cuddly HOWEVER hard I look. It's not in the Dark and Scary Wood and it's not under my pillow . . . You and Stanley must come and find it for me, because I just can't sleep without my *cuddly*."

So Emily Brown and Stanley put on their wet-weather wind-coats, and their see-in-the-dark glasses, and their special boots for climbing.

They searched down low in the tangles,

and they searched up high in the treetops.

GRRR!

They ran away from wolves,

and eventually they
found the Thing's cuddly,
right at the top of the
twistiest, thorniest tree in
the Dark and Scary
Wood.

and they lifted up trolls,

"Thank you," said the Thing.
"Don't mention it," said Emily Brown. "And now you must be quiet.
Stanley and I are TRYING to sleep."
"I promise," said the Thing, cuddling his cuddly.
Emily Brown shut the window.

A short while later, Emily Brown and Stanley were trying to get to sleep again.
But a noise was keeping them awake.
RUMBLE RUMBLE **RUMBLE** went the noise.
RUMBLE RUMBLE RUMBLE. RUMBLE! RUMBLE! RUMBLE!

It seemed to be coming from the kitchen.

"Oh, Emily Brown, Emily Brown!" grumbled the Thing. "ALL I had for tea was a hundred hamburgers and one small apple for the vitamins, and now I'm ever so hungry and thirsty . . . You and Stanley must fetch me my bedtime milk, because I just can't sleep when my tummy is rumbling."

So Emily Brown and Stanley sighed heavily, and put snow-snugglers on their heads, and ski-plankers on their feet, and their fluffiest winter-warmers over everything. They skied OFF through the Wild and Whirling Wastes, through blizzards and hurricanes, till their hands were frozen and their legs were sore, searching for a mug of milk for the Thing's bedtime snack.

Stanley had to distract a polar bear who thought the milk belonged to HIM.

"Thank you," said the Thing.

"Don't mention it," said Emily Brown. "And now you must be quiet. STANLEY AND I ARE *TRYING* TO SLEEP."

"I promise," said the Thing, dropping most of his milk over his pyjama top.

Emily
Brown
shut the
refrigerator
door.

Five minutes later, Emily Brown and Stanley were STILL trying to get to sleep.
But a noise was keeping them awake.
COUGH COUGH COUGH COUGH COUGH went the noise.
COUGH COUGH COUGH COUGH COUGH.
It seemed to be coming from the cellar door under the stairs.
"I hope it's not that Thing again," said Emily Brown, crossly.

It WAS the Thing.

"Oh, Emily Brown, Emily Brown!" coughed the Thing. "I'm feeling very poorly. I need my special green medicine . . . You and Stanley must fetch it for me from the Whiny Witches' Cavern, down under these stairs, because I just can't sleep when my throat is tickling."

So Emily Brown and Stanley gritted their teeth and pulled out their see-in-the-dark glasses again,

and their special tangly ropes, and their bottles for carrying medicine in.

They crept through

the twisty, turny Witches' Caverns under the stairs, and they put their hands on cobwebs,

THIS WAY

and they bumped into bats.

They had to tell the
Whiny Witches lots and
lots of stories in return
for the medicine.

"Thank you," said the Thing.
"Don't mention it," said Emily Brown.
"And now you really, really DO have to be quiet.
Stanley and I are . . . TRYING . . . to . . . sleep . . ."

Emily Brown had hardly even shut her eyes before the noise started again.
SCRATCH SCRATCH SCRATCH went the noise.

It seemed to be coming from under the bed.

It was that Thing again.
"I've got this very itchy leg . . ." began the Thing.

But this time Emily Brown had HAD ENOUGH.

"STOP!" shouted Emily Brown.

"I've HAD ENOUGH! We've *rescued* your cuddly from the Dark and Scary Wood! We've *fetched* your milk from the Wild and Whirling Wastes! We've *borrowed* your medicine from the Weird and Whiny Witches!

Stanley and I are EXHAUSTED. There's nothing wrong with your leg.

What's REALLY the matter?"

CLICK!

Two large tears crept down the Thing's cheeks and onto his furry chest.

"I'm *s-s-s-scared* . . . " whispered the Thing.

"Oh, so THAT'S been the problem," said Emily Brown, drying his tears and handing him his cuddly again.

"What are you *scared* OF?"

"Oh . . . I don't know. *Things* . . . " said the Thing.

"But YOU are a Thing," said Emily Brown.

"Am I?" said the Thing, in surprise. "I wondered what I was . . ."

"You're definitely a Thing," said Emily Brown, tucking him in tightly, and putting his hot-water bottle underneath his hairy legs.

CLICK!

"Am I scary?" asked the Thing.

"You're not at all scary," said Emily Brown.
"You're a very NICE Thing, and when Stanley and I are trying
to get to sleep we always find it helps to think of Nice Things.
Maybe you should try doing that yourself?"

"Maybe I will . . . " said the Nice Thing, yawning very wide.
"Night-night, Emily Brown . . . Sleep tight . . ."

" . . . Sweet dreams."